BALLET CAT

Dance! Dance! Underpants!

Bob Shea

SCHOLASTIC INC.

What do you mean? Super-high leaps are the best part of ballet.

Leaping seems like showing off. Pointing toes is classy.

What?
Super-high leaps
are what make ballet
so much fun.
They are not showy.
They are great.

And dangerous.

Look at that fancy light. A leaping bear could hurt her head on a fancy light like that.

Dangerous?

No problem.

That is where it was!

I am hungry. Will you pour me some cereal?

AHHH!
Okay, what do you want to drink? Orange juice?

No. What is hard to make and takes a long time?

Oh, my goodness,
you are right!

It is very late.

No wonder I am so
tired. I must go to
sleep for the winter.

See you in the spring,
Ballet Cat.

Whisper.
Whisper.
Whisper.

If you dance with all your heart, the only thing they will see is the beauty of ballet.

They will forget all about your underpants.

Leap, Butter Bear, leap!

Fantastic!

Lovely!

WOW!

Brava!

Applause!

Applause!

Applause!

Applause!

Hooray!
Ballet conquers all!